Nine O'Clock

Nine O'Clock

Wilkie Collins

MINT EDITIONS

Nine O'Clock was first published in 1852.

This edition published by Mint Editions 2021.

ISBN 9781513282206 | E-ISBN 9781513287225

Published by Mint Editions®

 MINT
EDITIONS
minteditionbooks.com

Publishing Director: Jennifer Newens
Design & Production: Rachel Lopez Metzger
Project Manager: Micaela Clark
Typesetting: Westchester Publishing Services

The night of the 30th of June, 1793, is memorable in the prison annals of Paris, as the last night in confinement of the leaders of the famous Girondin party in the first French revolution. On the morning of the 31st, the twenty-one deputies who represented the department of the Gironde, were guillotined to make way for Robespierre and the Reign of Terror.

With these men fell the last revolutionists of that period who shrank from founding a republic on massacre; who recoiled from substituting for a monarchy of corruption, a monarchy of bloodshed. The elements of their defeat lay as much in themselves, as in the events of their time. They were not, as a party, true to their own convictions; they temporized; they fatally attempted to take a middle course amid the terrible emergencies of a terrible epoch, and they fell—fell before worse men, because those men were in earnest.

Condemned to die, the Girondins submitted nobly to their fate; their great glory was the glory of their deaths. The speech of one of them on hearing his sentence pronounced, was a prophecy of the future, fulfilled to the letter.

"*I* die," he said to the Jacobin judges, the creatures of Robespierre, who tried him. "*I* die at a time when the people have lost their reason; *you* will die on the day when they recover it." Valazé was the only member of the condemned party who displayed a momentary weakness; he stabbed himself on hearing his sentence pronounced. But the blow was not mortal—he died on the scaffold, and died bravely with the rest.

On the night of the 30th the Girondins held their famous banquet in the prison; celebrated, with the ferocious stoicism of the time, their last social meeting before the morning on which they were to die. Other men, besides the twenty-one, were present at this supper of the condemned. They were prisoners who held Girondin opinions, but whose names were not illustrious enough for history to preserve. Though sentenced to confinement they were not sentenced to death. Some of their number, who had protested most boldly against the condemnation of the deputies, were ordered to witness the execution on the morrow, as a timely example to terrify them into submission. More than this, Robespierre and his colleagues did not, as yet, venture to attempt: the Reign of Terror was a cautious reign at starting.

The supper-table of the prison was spread; the guests, twenty-one of their number stamped already with the seal of death, were congregated at the last Girondin banquet; toast followed toast; the *Marseillaise* was sung; the desperate triumph of the feast was rising fast to its climax, when a new and ominous subject of conversation was started at the lower end of the table, and spread electrically, almost in a moment, to the top.

This subject (by whom originated no one knew) was simply a question as to the hour in the morning at which the execution was to take place. Every one of the prisoners appeared to be in ignorance on this point; and the gaolers either could not, or would not, enlighten them. Until the cart for the condemned rolled into the prison-yard, not one of the Girondins could tell whether he was to be called out to the guillotine soon after sunrise, or not till near noon.

This uncertainty was made a topic for discussion, or for jesting on all sides. It was eagerly seized on as a pretext for raising to the highest pitch the ghastly animation and hilarity of the evening. In some quarters, the recognised hour of former executions was quoted as precedent sure to be followed by the executioners of the morrow; in others, it was asserted that Robespierre and his party would purposely depart from established customs in this, as in previous instances. Dozens of wild schemes were suggested for guessing the hour by fortune-telling rules on the cards; bets were offered and accepted among the prisoners who were not condemned to death, and witnessed in stoical mockery by the prisoners who were. Jests were exchanged about early rising and hurried toilets; in short, every man contributed an assertion, with one solitary exception. That exception was the Girondin, Duprat, one of the deputies who was sentenced to die by the guillotine.

He was a younger man than the majority of his brethren, and was personally remarkable by his pale, handsome, melancholy face, and his reserved yet gentle manners. Throughout the evening, he had spoken but rarely; there was something of the silence and serenity of a martyr in his demeanour. That he feared death as little as any of his companions was plainly visible in his bright, steady eye; in his unchanging complexion; in his firm, calm voice, when he occasionally addressed those who happened to be near him. But he was evidently out of place at the banquet; his temperament was reflective, his disposition serious; feasts were at no time a sphere in which he was calculated to shine.

His taciturnity, while the hour of the execution was under discussion, had separated him from most of those with whom he sat, at the lower end of the table. They edged up towards the top, where the conversation was most general and most animated. One of his friends, however, still kept his place by Duprat's side, and thus questioned him anxiously, but in low tones, on the cause of his immovable silence:

"Are you the only man of the company, Duprat, who has neither a guess nor a joke to make about the time of the execution?"

"I never joke, Marginy," was the answer, given with a slight smile which had something of the sarcastic in it; "and as for guessing at the time of the execution, I never guess at things which I *know*."

"Know! You know the hour of the execution! Then why not communicate your knowledge to your friends around you?"

"Because not one of them would believe what I said."

"But, surely, you could prove it. Somebody must have told you."

"Nobody has told me."

"You have seen some private letter, then; or you have managed to get sight of the execution-order; or—"

"Spare your conjectures, Marginy. I have not read, as I have not been told, what is the hour at which we are to die to-morrow."

"Then how on earth can you possibly know it?"

"I do *not* know when the execution will begin, or when it will end. I only know that it will be *going on* at nine o'clock to-morrow morning. Out of the twenty-one who are to suffer death, one will be guillotined exactly at that hour. Whether he will be the first whose head falls, or the last, I cannot tell."

"And pray who may this man be, who is going to die exactly at nine o'clock? Of course, prophetically knowing so much, you know that!"

"I *do* know it. I am the man whose death by the guillotine will take place exactly at the hour I have mentioned."

"You said just now, Duprat, that you never joked. Do you expect me to believe that what you have just spoken is spoken in earnest?"

"I repeat that I never joke; and I answer that I expect you to believe me. I know the hour at which my death will take place tomorrow, just as certainly as I know the fact of my own existence tonight."

"But how? My dear friend, can you really lay claim to supernatural intuition, in this eighteenth century of the world, in this renowned Age of reason?"

"No two men, Marginy, understand that word, supernatural, exactly in the same sense; you and I differ about its meaning, or, in other words, differ about the real distinction between the doubtful and the true. We will not discuss the subject: I wish to be understood, at the outset, as laying claim to no superior intuitions whatever; but I tell you, at the same time, that even in this Age of Reason, I have reason for what I have said. My father and my brother both died at nine o'clock in the morning, and were both warned very strangely of their deaths. I am the last of my family; I was warned last night, as they were warned; and I shall die by the guillotine, as they died in their beds, at the fatal hour of nine."

"But, Duprat, why have I never heard of this before? As your oldest and, I am sure, your dearest friend, I thought you had long since trusted me with all your secrets."

"And you shall know this secret; I only kept it from you till the time when I would be certain that my death would substantiate my words, to the very letter. Come! you are as bad supper-company as I am; let us slip away from the table unperceived, while our friends are all engaged in conversation. Yonder end of the hall is dark and quiet—we can speak there uninterruptedly, for some hours to come,"

He led the way from the supper-table, followed by Marginy. Arrived at one of the darkest and most retired corners of the great hall of the prison, Duprat spoke again:

"I believe, Marginy," he said, "that you are one of those who have been ordered by our tyrants to witness my execution, and the execution of my brethren, as a warning spectacle for an enemy to the Jacobin cause?"

"My dear, dear friend! it is too true; I am ordered to witness the butchery which I cannot prevent—our last awful parting will be at the foot of the scaffold. I am among the victims who are spared—mercilessly spared—for a little while yet."

"Say the martyrs! We die as martyrs, calmly, hopefully, innocently. When I am placed under the guillotine to-morrow morning, listen, my friend, for the striking of the church clocks; listen for the hour while you look your last on me. Until that time, suspend your judgement on the strange chapter of family history which I am now about to relate."

Marginy took his friend's hand, and promised compliance with the request. Duprat then began as follows:

"You knew my brother Alfred, when he was quite a youth, and you knew something of what people flippantly termed, the eccentricities of his character. He was three years my junior; but from childhood, he showed far less of a child's innate levity and happiness than his elder brother. He was noted for his seriousness and thoughtfulness as a boy; showed little inclination for a boy's usual lessons, and less still for a boy's usual recreations,—in short, he was considered by everybody (my father included) as deficient in intellect; as a vacant dreamer, and an inveterate idler, whom it was hopeless to improve. our tutor tried to lead him to various studies, and tried in vain. It was the same when the cultivation of his mind was given up, and the cultivation of his body was next attempted. The fencing-master could make nothing of him; and the dancing-master, after the first three lessons, resigned in despair. Seeing that it was useless to set others to teach him, my father made a virtue of necessity, and left him, if he chose, to teach himself.

"To the astonishment of every one, he had not been long consigned to his own guidance, when he was discovered in the library, reading every old treatise on astrology which he could lay his hands on. He had rejected all useful knowledge for the most obsolete of obsolete sciences—the old, abandoned delusion of divination by stars! My father laughed heartily over the strange study to which his idle son had at last applied himself, but made no attempt to oppose his new caprice, and sarcastically presented him with a telescope on his next birthday. I should remind you here, of what you may perhaps have forgotten, that my father was a philosopher of the Voltaire school, who believed that the summit of human wisdom was to arrive at the power of sneering at all enthusiasms, and doubting of all truths. Apart from his philosophy, he was a kind-hearted, easy man, of quick, rather than profound intelligence. He could see nothing in my brother's new occupation, but the evidence of a new idleness, a fresh caprice which would be abandoned in a few months. My father was not the man to appreciate those yearnings towards the poetical and the spiritual, which were part of Alfred's temperament, and which gave to his peculiar studies of the stars and their influences, a certain charm altogether unconnected with the more practical attractions of scientific investigation.

"This idle caprice of my brother's, as my father insisted on terming it, had lasted more than a twelvemonth, when there occurred the first of a series of mysterious and—as I consider them—supernatural events, with all of which Alfred was very remarkably connected. I was myself a witness of the strange circumstance, which I am now about to relate to you.

"One day—my brother being then sixteen years of age—I happened to go into my father's study, during his absence, and found Alfred there, standing close to a window, which looked into the garden. I walked up to him, and observed a curious expression of vacancy and rigidity in his face, especially in his eyes. Although I knew him to be subject to what are called fits of absence, I still thought it rather extraordinary that he never moved, and never noticed me when I was close to him. I took his hand, and asked if he was unwell. his flesh felt quite cold; neither my touch nor my voice produced the smallest sensation in him. Almost at the same moment when I noticed this, I happened to be looking accidentally towards the garden. There was my father walking along one of the paths, and there, by his side, walking with him, was *another Alfred!*—Another, yet exactly the same as the Alfred by whose side I was standing, whose hand I still held in mine!

"Thoroughly panic-stricken, I dropped his hand, and uttered a cry of terror. At the loud sound of my voice, the statue-like presence before me immediately began to show signs of animation. I looked round again at the garden. The figure of my brother, which I had beheld there, was gone, and I saw to my horror, that my father was looking for it—looking in all directions for the companion (spectre, or human being?) of his walk!

"When I turned towards Alfred once more, he had (if I may so express it) come to life again, and was asking, with his usual gentleness of manner and kindness of voice, why I was looking so pale? I evaded the question by making some excuse, and in my turn inquired of him, how long he had been in my father's study.

"'Surely you ought to know best,' he answered with a laugh, 'for you must have been here before me. It is not many minutes ago since I was walking in the garden with—'

"Before he could complete the sentence my father entered the room.

"'Oh! here you are, Master Alfred,' said he. 'May I ask for what purpose you took it into your wise head to vanish in that extraordinary manner? Why you slipped away from me in an instant, while I was picking a flower! On my word, sir, you're a better player at hide-and-seek than your brother,—*he* would only have run into the shrubbery, *you* have managed to run in here, though how you did it in the time passes my poor comprehension. I was not a moment picking the flower, yet in that moment you were gone!'

"Alfred glanced suddenly and searchingly at me; his face became deadly pale, and, without speaking a word, he hurried from the room.

"'Can *you* explain this?' said my father, looking very much astonished.

"I hesitated a moment, and then told him what I had seen. He took a pinch of snuff—a favourite habit with him when he was going to be sarcastic, in imitation of Voltaire.

"'One visionary in a family is enough,' said he; 'I recommend you not to turn yourself into a bad imitation of your brother Alfred! Send your ghost after me, my good boy! I am going back into the garden, and should like to see him again!'

"Ridicule, even much sharper than this, would have had little effect on me. If I was certain of anything in the world, I was certain that I had seen my brother in the study—nay, more, had touched him,—and equally certain that I had seen his double—his exact similitude, in the garden. As far as any man could know that he was in possession of his own senses, I knew myself to be in possession of mine. Left alone to think over what I had beheld, I felt a supernatural terror creeping through me—a terror which increased, when I recollected that, on one or two occasions friends had said they had seen Alfred out of doors, when we all knew him to be at home. These statements, which my father had laughed at, and had taught me to laugh at, either as a trick, or a delusion on the part of others, now recurred to my memory as startling corroborations of what I had just seen myself. The solitude of the study oppressed me in a manner which I cannot describe. I left the apartment to seek Alfred, determined to question him, with all possible caution, on the subject of his strange trance, and his sensations at the moment when I had awakened him from it.

"I found him in his bed-room, still pale, and now very thoughtful. As the first words in reference to the scene in the study passed my lips, he started violently, and entreated me, with very unusual warmth of speech and manner, never to speak to him on that subject again,—never, if I had any love or regard for him! Of course, I complied with his request. The mystery, however, was not destined to end here.

"About two months after the event which I have just related, we had arranged, one evening, to go to the theatre. My father had insisted that Alfred should be of the party, otherwise he would certainly have declined accompanying us; for he had no inclination whatever for public amusements of any kind. However, with his usual docility, he prepared to obey my father's desire, by going up-stairs to put on his evening dress. It was winter-time, so he was obliged to take a candle with him.

"We waited in the drawing-room for his return a very long time, so long, that my father was on the point of sending up-stairs to remind him of the lateness of the hour, when Alfred reappeared without the candle which he had taken with him from the room. The ghostly alteration over his face—the hideous, death-look that distorted his features I shall never forget,—I shall see it to-morrow on the scaffold!

"Before either my father or I could utter a word, my brother said: 'I have been taken suddenly ill; but I am better now. Do you still wish me to go to the theatre?'

"'Certainly not, my dear Alfred,' answered my father; 'we must send for the doctor immediately.'

"'Pray do not call in the doctor, sir; he would be of no use. I will tell you why, if you will let me speak to you alone.'

"My father, looking seriously alarmed, signed to me to leave the room. For more than half an hour I remained absent, suffering almost unendurable suspense and anxiety on my brother's account. When I was recalled, I observed that Alfred was quite calm, though still deadly pale. My father's manner displayed an agitation which I had never observed in it before. He rose from his chair when I re-entered the room, and left me alone with my brother.

"'Promise me,' said Alfred, in answer to my entreaties to know what had happened, 'promise that you will not ask me to tell you more than my father has permitted me to tell. It is his desire that I should keep certain things a secret from you.'

"I gave the required promise, but gave it most unwillingly. Alfred then proceeded.

"'When I left you to go and dress for the theatre, I felt a sense of oppression all over me, which I cannot describe. As soon as I was alone, it seemed as if some part of the life within me was slowly wasting away. I could hardly breathe the air around me, big drops of perspiration burst out on my forehead, and then a feeling of terror seized me which I was utterly unable to control. Some of those strange fancies of seeing my mother's spirit, which used to influence me at the time of her death, came back again to my mind. I ascended the stairs slowly and painfully, not daring to look behind me, for I heard—yes, heard!—something following me. When I got into my room, and had shut the door, I began to recover my self-possession a little. But the sense of oppression was still as heavy on me as ever, when I approached the wardrobe to get out my clothes. Just as I stretched forth my hand to turn the key, I saw, to my horror, the two doors of the wardrobe opening of themselves, opening slowly and silently. The candle went out at the same moment, and the whole inside of the wardrobe became to me like a great mirror, with a bright light shining in the middle of it. Out of that light there came a figure, the exact counterpart of myself. Over its breast hung an open scroll, and on that I read the warning of my own death, and a revelation of the destinies of my father and his race. Do not ask me what were the words on the scroll, I have given my promise not to tell you. I may only say that, as soon as I had read all, the room grew dark, and the vision disappeared.'

"Forgetful of my promise, I entreated Alfred to repeat to me the words on the scroll. He smiled sadly, and refused to speak on the subject any more. I next sought out my father, and begged him to divulge the secret. Still sceptical to the last, he answered that one diseased imagination in the family was enough, and that he would not permit me to run the risk of being infected by Alfred's mental malady. I passed the whole of that day and the next in a state of agitation and alarm which nothing could tranquilise. The sight I had seen in the study gave a terrible significance to the little that my brother had told me. I was uneasy if he was a moment out of my sight. There was something in his expression,—calm and even cheerful as it was,—which made me dread the worst.

"On the morning of the third day after the occurrence I have just related, I rose very early, after a sleepless night, and went into Alfred's bedroom. He was awake, and welcomed me with more than usual affection and kindness. As I drew a chair to his bedside, he asked me to get pen, ink, and paper, and write down something from his dictation. I obeyed, and found to my terror and distress, that the idea of death was more present to his imagination than ever. He employed me in writing a statement of his wishes in regard to the disposal of all his own little possessions, as keepsakes to be given, after he was no more, to my father, myself, the house-servants, and one or two of his own most intimate friends. Over and over again I entreated him to tell me whether he really believed that his death was near. He invariably replied that I should soon know, and then led the conversation to indifferent topics. As the morning advanced, he asked to see my father, who came, accompanied by the doctor, the latter having been in attendance for the last two days.

"Alfred took my father's hand, and begged his forgiveness of any offence, any disobedience of which he had ever been guilty. Then, reaching out his other hand, and taking mine, as I stood on the opposite side of the bed, he asked what the time was. A clock was placed on the mantel-piece of the room, but not in a position in which he could see it, as he now lay. I turned round to look at the dial, and answered that, it was just on the stroke of nine.

"'Farewell!' said Alfred, calmly; 'in this world, farewell for ever!'

"The next instant the clock struck. I felt his fingers tremble in mine, then grow quite still. The doctor seized a hand-mirror that lay on the table, and held it over his lips. He was dead—dead, as the last chime of the hour echoed through the awful silence of the room!

"I pass over the first days of our affliction. You, who have suffered the loss of a beloved sister, can well imagine their misery. I pass over these days, and pause for a moment at the time when we could speak with some calmness and resignation on the subject of our bereavement. On the arrival of that period, I ventured, in conversation with my father, to refer to the vision which had been seen by our dear Alfred in his bedroom, and to the prophecy which he described himself as having read upon the supernatural scroll.

"Even yet my father persisted in his scepticism; but now, as it seemed to me, more because he was afraid, than because he was unwilling, to believe. I again recalled to his memory what I myself had seen in the study. I asked him to recollect how certain Alfred had been beforehand, and how fatally right, about the day and hour of his death. Still I could get but one answer; my brother had died of a nervous disorder (the doctor said so); his imagination had been diseased from his childhood; there was only one way of treating the vision which he described himself as having seen, and that was, not to speak of it again between ourselves; never to speak of it at all to our friends.

"We were sitting in the study during this conversation. It was evening. As my father uttered the last words of his reply to me, I saw his eye turn suddenly and uneasily towards the further end of the room. In dead silence, I looked in the same direction, and saw the door opening of itself. the vacant space beyond was filled with a bright, steady glow, which hid all outer objects in the hall, and which I cannot describe to you by likening it to any light that we are accustomed to behold either by day or night. In my terror, I caught my father by the arm, and asked him, in a whisper, whether he did not see something extraordinary in the direction of the doorway?

"'Yes,' he answered, in tones as low as mine, 'I see, or fancy I see, a strange light. The subject on which we have been speaking has impressed our feelings as it should not. Our nerves are still unstrung by the shock of the bereavement we have suffered: our senses are deluding us. Let us look away towards the garden.'

"'But the opening of the door, father; remember the opening of the door!'

"'Ours is not the first door which has accidentally flown open of itself.'

"'Then why not shut it again?'

"'Why not, indeed. I will close it at once.' He rose, advanced a few paces, then stopped, and came back to his place. 'It is a warm evening,' he said, avoiding my eyes, which were eagerly fixed on him, 'the room will be all the cooler, if the door is suffered to remain open.'

"His face grew quite pale as he spoke. The light lasted for a few minutes longer, then suddenly disappeared. For the rest of the evening my father's manner was very much altered. He was silent and thoughtful, and complained of a feeling of oppression and languor, which he tried to persuade himself was produced by the heat of the weather. At an unusually hour he retired to his room.

"The next morning, when I got down stairs, I found, to my astonishment, that the servants were engaged in preparations for the departure of somebody from the house. I made inquiries of one of them who was hurriedly packing a trunk. 'My master, sir, starts for Lyons the first thing this morning,' was the reply. I immediately repaired to my father's room, and found him there with an open letter in his hand, which he was reading. His face, as he looked up at me on my entrance, expressed the most violent emotions of apprehension and despair.

"'I hardly know whether I am awake or dreaming; whether I am the dupe of a terrible delusion, or the victim of a supernatural reality more terrible still,' he said in low awe-struck tones as I approached him. 'One of the prophecies which Alfred told me in private that he had read upon the scroll, has come true! He predicted the loss of the bulk of my fortune—here is the letter, which informs me that the merchant at Lyons in whose hands my money was placed, has become bankrupt. Can the occurrence of this ruinous calamity be the chance fulfilment of a mere guess? Or was the doom of my family really revealed to my dead son? I go to Lyons immediately to know the truth: this letter may have been written under false information; it may be the work of an impostor. And yet, Alfred's prediction—I shudder to think of it!'

"'The light, father!' I exclaimed, 'the light we saw last night in the study!'

"'Hush! don't speak of it! Alfred said that I should be warned of the truth of the prophecy, and of its immediate fulfilment, by the shining of the same supernatural light that he had seen—I tried to disbelieve what I beheld last night—I hardly know whether I dare believe it even now!

This prophecy is not the last: there are others yet to be fulfilled—but let us not speak, let us not think of them! I must start at once for Lyons; I must be on the spot, if this horrible news is true, to save what I can from the wreck. The letter—give me back the letter!—I must go directly!'

"He hurried back from the room. I followed him; and, with some difficulty, obtained permission to be the companion of his momentous journey. When we arrived at Lyons, we found that the statement in the letter was true. My father's fortune was gone: a mere pittance, derived from a small estate that had belonged to my mother, was all that was left to us.

"My father's health gave way under this misfortune. He never referred again to Alfred's prediction, and I was afraid to mention the subject; but I saw that it was affecting his mind quite as painfully as the loss of his property. Over, and over again, he checked himself very strangely when he was on the point of speaking to me about my brother. I saw that there was some secret pressing heavily on his mind, which he was afraid to disclose to me. It was useless to ask for his confidence. His temper had become irritable under disaster; perhaps, also, under the dread uncertainties which were now evidently tormenting him in secret. My situation was a very sad, and a very dreary one, at that time: I had no remembrances of the past that were not mournful and affrighting remembrances; I had no hopes for the future that were not darkened by a vague presentiment of troubles and perils to come; and I was expressly forbidden by my father to say a word about the terrible events which had cast an unnatural gloom over my youthful career, to any of the friends (yourself included) whose counsel and whose sympathy might have guided and sustained me in the day of trial.

"We returned to Paris; sold our house there; and retired to live on the small estate, to which I have referred, as the last possession left us. We had not been many days in our new abode, when my father imprudently exposed himself to a heavy shower of rain, and suffered in consequence from a violent attack of cold. This temporary malady was not dreaded by the medical attendant; but it was soon aggravated by a fever, produced as much by the anxiety and distress of mind from which he continued to suffer, as by any other cause. Still the doctor gave hope; but still he grew daily worse—so much worse, that I removed my bed into his room, and never quitted him night or day.

"One night I had fallen asleep, overpowered by fatigue and anxiety, when I was awakened by a cry from my father. I instantly trimmed the light, and ran to his side. He was sitting up in bed, with his eyes fixed on the door, which had been left ajar to ventilate the room. I saw nothing in that direction, and asked what was the matter. He murmured some expressions of affection towards me, and begged me to sit by his bedside till the morning; but gave no definite answer to my question. Once or twice, I thought he wandered a little; and I observed that he occasionally moved his hand under the pillow, as if searching for something there. However, when the morning came, he appeared to be calm and self-possessed. The doctor arrived; and pronouncing him to be better, retired to the dressing-room to write a prescription. The moment his back was turned, my father laid his weak hand on my arm, and whispered faintly: 'Last night I saw the supernatural light again—the second prediction—true, true—my death this time—the same hour as Alfred's—nine—nine o'clock, this morning.' He paused a moment through weakness; then added: 'Take that sealed paper—under the pillow—when I am dead, read it—now go into the dressing-room—my watch is there—I have heard the church clock strike eight; let me see how long it is now till nine—go—go quickly!'

"Horror-stricken, moving and acting like a man in a trance, I silently obeyed him. The doctor was still in the dressing-room: despair made me catch eagerly at any chance of saving my father; I told his medical attendant what I had just heard, and entreated advice and assistance without delay.

"'He is a little delirious,' said the doctor—'don't be alarmed: we can cheat him out of his dangerous idea, and so perhaps save his life. Where is the watch?' (I produced it)—'See: it is ten minutes to nine. I will put back the hands one hour; that will give good time for a composing draught to operate. There! take him the watch, and let him see the false time with his own eyes. He will be comfortably asleep before the hour hand gets round again to nine.'

"I went back with the watch to my father's bed-side. 'Too slow,' he murmured, as he looked at the dial—'too slow by an hour—the church clock—I counted eight.'

"'Father! dear father! you are mistaken,' I cried, '*I* counted also: it was only seven.'

"'Only seven!' he echoed faintly, 'another hour then—another hour to live!' He evidently believed what I had said to him. In spite of the fatal experiences of the past, I now ventured to hope the best for our stratagem, as I resumed my place by his side.

"The doctor came in; but my father never noticed him. He kept his eyes fixed on the watch, which lay between us, on the coverlid. When the minute hand was within a few seconds of indicating the false hour of eight, he looked round at me, murmured very feebly and doubtingly, 'another hour to live!' and then gently closed his eyes. I looked at the watch, and saw that it was just eight o'clock, according to our alteration of the right time. At the same moment, I heard the doctor, whose hand had been on my father's pulse, exclaim, 'My God! it's stopped! He *has* died at nine o'clock!'

"The fatality, which no human stratagem or human science could turn aside, was accomplished! I was alone in the world!

"In the solitude of our little cottage, on the day of my father's burial, I opened the sealed letter, which he had told me to take from the pillow of his death-bed. In preparing to read it, I knew that I was preparing for the knowledge of my own doom; but I neither trembled nor wept. I was beyond grief: despair such as mine was then, is calm and self-possessed to the last.

"The letter ran thus: 'After your father and brother have fallen under the fatality that pursues our house, it is right, my dear son, that you should be warned how *you* are included in the last of the predictions which still remains unaccomplished. Know then, that the final lines read by our dear Alfred on the scroll, prophesied that *you* should die, as *we* have died, at the fatal hour of nine; but by a bloody and violent death, the day of which was not foretold. My beloved boy! you know not, you never will know, what I suffered in the possession of this terrible secret, as the truth of the former prophecies forced itself more and more plainly on my mind! Even now, as I write, I hope against all hope; believe vainly and desperately against all experience, that this last, worst doom may be avoided. Be cautious; be patient; look well before you at each step of your career. The fatality by which you are threatened is terrible; but there is a Power above fatality; and before that Power my spirit and my child's spirit now pray for you. Remember this when your heart is heavy, your path through life grows dark. Remember that the better world is still before you, the world where we shall all meet! Farewell!'

"When I first read those lines, I read them with the gloomy, immovable resignation of the Eastern fatalists; and that resignation never left me afterwards. Here, in this prison, I feel it, calm as ever. I bowed patiently to my doom, when it was only predicted: I bow to it as

WILKIE COLLINS

patiently now, when it is on the eve of accomplishment. You have often wondered, my friend, at the tranquil, equable sadness of my manner: after what I have just told you, can you wonder any longer?

"But let me return for a moment to the past. Though I had no hope of escaping the fatality which had overtaken my father and my brother, my life, after my double bereavement, was the existence of all others which might seem most likely to evade the accomplishment of my predicted doom. Yourself and one other friend excepted, I saw no society; my walks were limited to the cottage garden and the neighbouring fields, and my every-day, unvarying occupation was confined to that hard and resolute course of study, by which alone I could hope to prevent my mind from dwelling on what I had suffered in the past, or on what I might still be condemned to suffer in the future. Never was there a life more quiet and more uneventful than mine!

"You know how I awoke to an ambition, which irresistibly impelled me to change this mode of existence. News from Paris penetrated even to my obscure retreat, and disturbed my self-imposed tranquility. I heard of the last errors and weaknesses of Louis the Sixteenth; I heard of the assembling of the States-General; and I knew that the French Revolution had begun. The tremendous emergencies of that epoch drew men of all characters from private to public pursuits, and made politics the necessity rather than the choice of every Frenchman's life. The great change preparing for the country acted universally on individuals, even to the humblest, and it acted on *me*.

"I was elected a deputy, more for the sake of the name I bore, than on account of any little influence which my acquirements and my character might have exercised in the neighbourhood of my country abode. I removed to Paris, and took my seat in the Chamber, little thinking at that time, of the crime and the bloodshed to which our revolution, so moderate in its beginning, would lead; little thinking that I had taken the first, irretrievable steps towards the bloody and violent death which was lying in store for me.

"Need I go on? You know how warmly I joined the Girondin party; you know how we have been sacrificed; you know what the death is which I and my brethren are to suffer to-morrow. On now ending, I repeat what I said at beginning: Judge not of my narrative till you have seen with your own eyes what really takes place in the morning. I have carefully abstained from all comment, I have simply related events as they happened, forbearing to add my own views of their significance, my own ideas on the explanation of which they admit. You may believe us to have been a family of nervous visionaries, witnesses of certain remarkable contingencies; victims of curious, but not impossible chances, which we have fancifully and falsely interpreted into supernatural events. I leave you undisturbed in this conviction (if you really feel it); to-morrow you will think differently; to-morrow you will be an altered man. In the mean time, remember what I now say, as you would remember my dying words: Last night I saw the supernatural radiance which warned my father and my brother; and which warns *me*, that, whatever the time when the execution begins, whatever the order in which the twenty-one Girondins are chosen for death, I shall be the man who kneels under the guillotine, as the clock strikes nine!"

It was morning. Of the ghastly festivities of the night no sign remained. The prison-hall wore an altered look, as the twenty-one condemned men (followed by those who were ordered to witness their execution) were marched out to the carts appointed to take them from the dungeon to the scaffold.

The sky was cloudless, the sun warm and brilliant, as the Girondin leaders and their companions were drawn slowly through the streets to the place of execution. Duprat and Marginy were placed in separate vehicles: the contrast in their demeanour at that awful moment was strongly marked. The features of the doomed man still preserved their noble and melancholy repose; his glance was steady; his colour never changed. The face of Marginy, on the contrary, displayed the strongest agitation; he was pale even to his lips. The terrible narrative he had heard, the anticipation of the final and appalling proof by which its truth was now to be tested, had robbed him, for the first time in his life, of all his self-possession. Duprat had predicted truly; the morrow had come, and he was an altered man already.

The carts drew up at the foot of the scaffold which was soon to be stained with the blood of twenty-one human beings. The condemned deputies mounted it; and ranged themselves at the end opposite the guillotine. The prisoners who were to behold the execution remained in their cart. Before Duprat ascended the steps, he friend's hand for the last time: "Farewell!" he said, calmly. "Farewell! I go to my father, and my brother! Remember my words of last night."

With straining eyes, and bloodless cheeks, Marginy saw Duprat take his position in the middle row of his companions, who stood in three ranks of seven each. Then the awful spectacle of the execution began. After the first seven deputies had suffered there was a pause; the horrible traces of the judicial massacre were being removed. When the execution proceeded, Duprat was the third taken from the middle rank of the condemned. As he came forward, he stood for an instant erect under the guillotine, he looked with a smile on his friend, and repeated in a clear voice the word, *"Remember!"*—then bowed himself on the block. The blood stood still at Marginy's heart, as he looked and listened, during the moment of silence that followed. That moment past, the church clocks of Paris struck. He dropped down in the cart, and covered his face with his hands; for through the heavy beat of the hour he heard the fall of the fatal steel.

"Pray, sir, was it nine or ten that struck just now?" said one of Marginy's fellow-prisoners to an officer of the guard who stood near the cart.

The person addressed referred to his watch, and answered—

"NINE O'CLOCK!"

A Note About the Author

Wilkie Collins (1824–1889) was an English novelist and playwright. Born in London, Collins was raised in England, Italy, and France by William Collins, a renowned landscape painter, and his wife Harriet Geddes. After working for a short time as a tea merchant, he published *Antonina* (1850), his literary debut. He quickly became known as a leading author of sensation novels, a popular genre now recognized as a forerunner to detective fiction. Encouraged on by the success of his early work, Collins made a name for himself on the London literary scene. He soon befriended Charles Dickens, forming a strong bond grounded in friendship and mentorship that would last several decades. His novels *The Woman in White* (1859) and *The Moonstone* (1868) are considered pioneering examples of mystery and detective fiction, and enabled Collins to become financially secure. Toward the end of the 1860s, at the height of his career, Collins began to suffer from numerous illnesses, including gout and opium addiction, which contributed to his decline as a writer. Beyond his literary work, Collins is seen as an early advocate for marriage reform, criticizing the institution and living a radically open romantic lifestyle.

A Note from the Publisher

Spanning many genres, from non-fiction essays to literature classics to children's books and lyric poetry, Mint Edition books showcase the master works of our time in a modern new package. The text is freshly typeset, is clean and easy to read, and features a new note about the author in each volume. Many books also include exclusive new introductory material. Every book boasts a striking new cover, which makes it as appropriate for collecting as it is for gift giving. Mint Edition books are only printed when a reader orders them, so natural resources are not wasted. We're proud that our books are never manufactured in excess and exist only in the exact quantity they need to be read and enjoyed.

Discover more of your favorite classics with Bookfinity™.

- Track your reading with custom book lists.
- Get great book recommendations for your personalized Reader Type.
- Add reviews for your favorite books.
- AND MUCH MORE!

Visit **bookfinity.com** and take the fun Reader Type quiz to get started.

Enjoy our classic and modern companion pairings!

www.ingramcontent.com/pod-product-compliance
Lightning Source LLC
Chambersburg PA
CBHW020614130626
46552CB00007B/3208